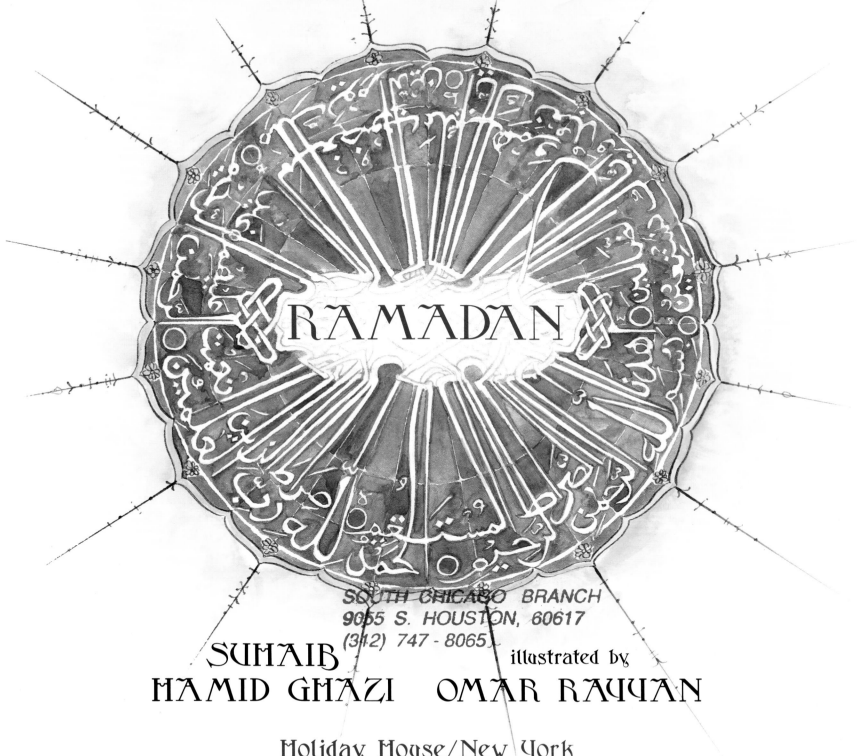

RAMADAN

SUHAIB
HAMID GHAZI

illustrated by
OMAR RAYYAN

Holiday House/New York

Library of Congress Cataloging-in-Publication Data
Ghazi, Suhaib Hamid.
Ramadan / Suhaib Hamid Ghazi; illustrated by Omar Rayyan. — 1st ed.
p.   cm.
Summary: Describes the celebration of the month of Ramadan by an
Islamic family and discusses the meaning and importance of this
holiday in the Islamic religion.
ISBN 0-8234-1254-7 (hardcover: alk. paper)
1. Ramadan — Juvenile literature. [1. Ramadan. 2. Fasts and
feasts — Islam. 3. Islam — Customs and practices.] I. Rayyan, Omar,
ill. II. Title.
BP186.4.G43   1996   96-5154   CIP   AC
297′.36 — dc20
ISBN 0-8234-1275-X (pbk.)

Assalamu alaikum! That means "May peace be upon you." Hakeem is a Muslim, which means that he believes in the religion of Islam. Islam is an Arabic word meaning peace and submission. All Muslims believe in one God called Allah.

Islam is a religion that is more than 1,400 years old and has many followers all around the globe. In fact, there are at least one billion Muslims in the world today. Muslims can be found in every country of the world, from America to Saudi Arabia, from India to Russia, from China to South Africa, and from France to Brazil.

Muslims have their own calendar which uses the moon to determine the length of months and the year. A calendar that uses the moon instead of the sun is called a lunar calendar. To find out when there is a new lunar month, look at the sky at night. When the thin crescent of a new moon can be seen for the first time, a new lunar month has started.

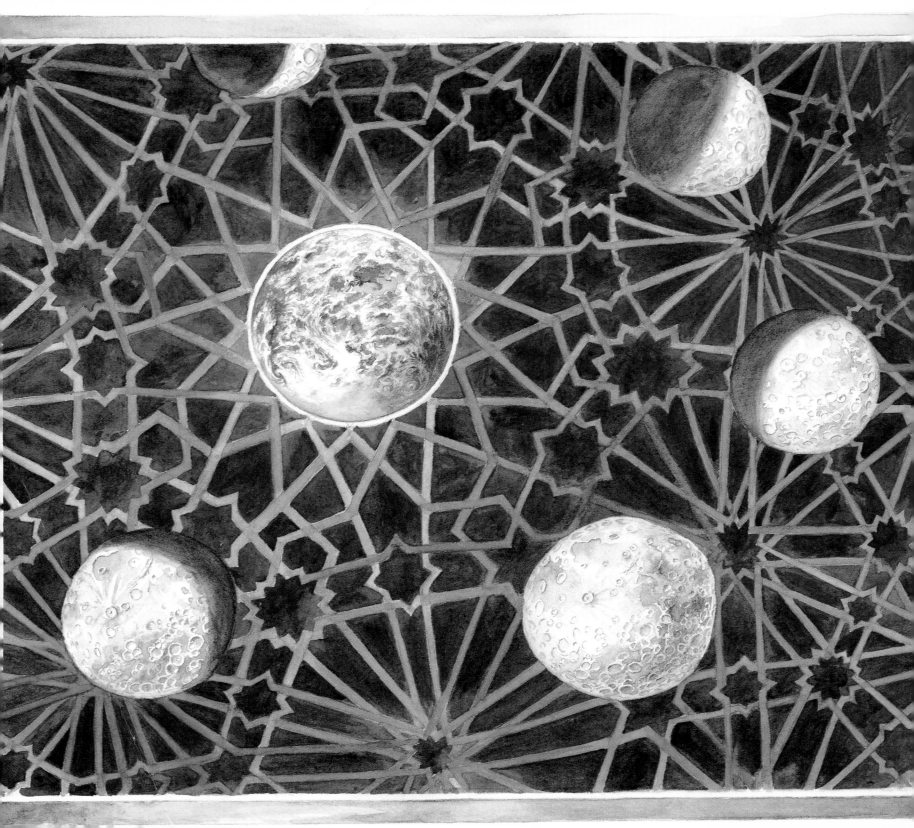

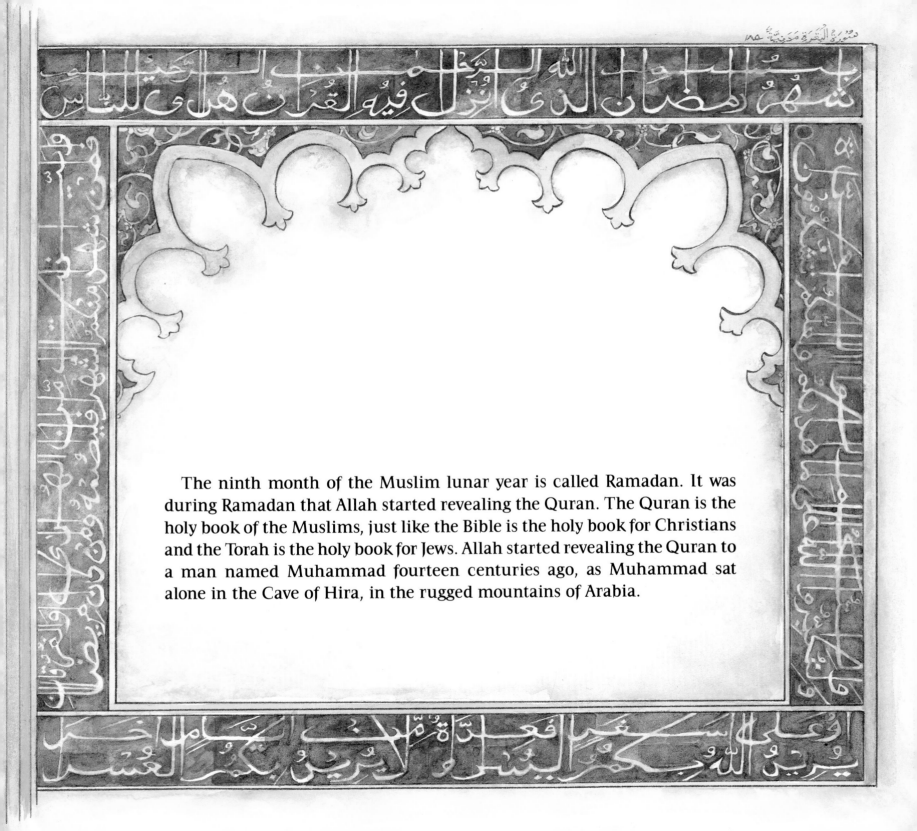

The ninth month of the Muslim lunar year is called Ramadan. It was during Ramadan that Allah started revealing the Quran. The Quran is the holy book of the Muslims, just like the Bible is the holy book for Christians and the Torah is the holy book for Jews. Allah started revealing the Quran to a man named Muhammad fourteen centuries ago, as Muhammad sat alone in the Cave of Hira, in the rugged mountains of Arabia.

Muslims all around the world eagerly wait for the month of Ramadan to arrive. On the twenty-seventh night of the eighth month, called Sha'aban, Hakeem's parents take him and his brother and sister to the hills by their house. There they scan the skies in the open air, looking for the thin crescent of a new moon. If they do not see it, they go back home and return the next night.

On the night that they finally see the slender slice of the new moon, they point to it and exclaim, "There it is! *Ramadan Mubarak*, everybody!"

This means "Have a blessed and happy Ramadan." It is the Muslims' way of congratulating each other on the beginning of the most special month of the Muslim year.

During Ramadan, Muslims around the world will fast all day long. From the moment the sun rises, Hakeem and his family will not eat or drink anything until the sun is fully set. They will not be allowed to put anything in their mouths, even such things as chewing gum or cigarettes. Many religions have one or two days during which the followers must fast. But in Islam, the followers must fast every day for a whole month.

To prepare for a day of fasting, Muslims wake up before dawn, when the sun has not yet risen and the whole world seems to be in bed. Even the roosters are still asleep. Families gather together and eat an early meal called *Suhur*. This meal will give them the energy and the nutrition they need to make it through the day without food.

Hakeem's family eats a variety of food during Suhur, from sweet, juicy fruits to delicious frosted pastries. His mother makes heaps of buttery scrambled eggs with toast and stacks of hot, fluffy pancakes smothered in thick maple syrup. Sometimes the family eats hot oatmeal with fresh berries and cream. When all are done eating, they wash their Suhur down with ice-cold milk or freshly squeezed orange juice to keep them healthy and strong.

Muslims are allowed to eat until the break of dawn, when there is enough light to see the difference between a black thread and a white thread. At that point, they recite together a prayer that states that they plan to fast for the whole day.

Then they wash themselves and perform the morning prayer together. This morning prayer is called *Fajr*, and it is the first of five daily prayers. Hakeem's father leads the prayer and the rest of the family follows him. When the prayer is done, Hakeem sometimes reads part of the Holy Quran with his parents. If he is tired, he goes back to bed for a couple of hours to get some more sleep.

Throughout the whole day, Muslims will not eat or drink anything. For the first few hours, this is easy for Hakeem because his stomach is full from Suhur, but during the middle of the day, he begins to feel a little bit hungry since he is used to having lunch.

If Ramadan is during the school year, Hakeem and his Muslim friends skip lunch and play outside. Playing usually keeps their minds off food. But they don't play too hard because they do not want to get thirsty.

By the time the evening comes around, Hakeem's stomach is rolling and grumbling for something to eat. The hardest part of fasting is the last few hours before sunset. It sometimes feels like the sun is stuck and has stopped moving. For Hakeem, those last few hours seem to take forever.

Ramadan is more than just a month of fasting. It is a month during which Muslims try to clean and purify their bodies and their minds. They try to spend as much time as possible reading the Holy Quran and saying prayers. They try to help people in need, whether they are friends, family, or people whom they do not even know.

Islam teaches them to be loving and caring with each other, as well as with people who are not Muslim. There must not be any arguing, fighting, or bad language. Ramadan is a time to end past arguments. Muslims say they are sorry to those they have hurt and forgive those people who have hurt them.

Ramadan also shows Muslims what it is like to be poor and hungry. As their stomachs roll and growl with hunger, they realize how the poor must feel every day. They become thankful and happy with what Allah has given them.

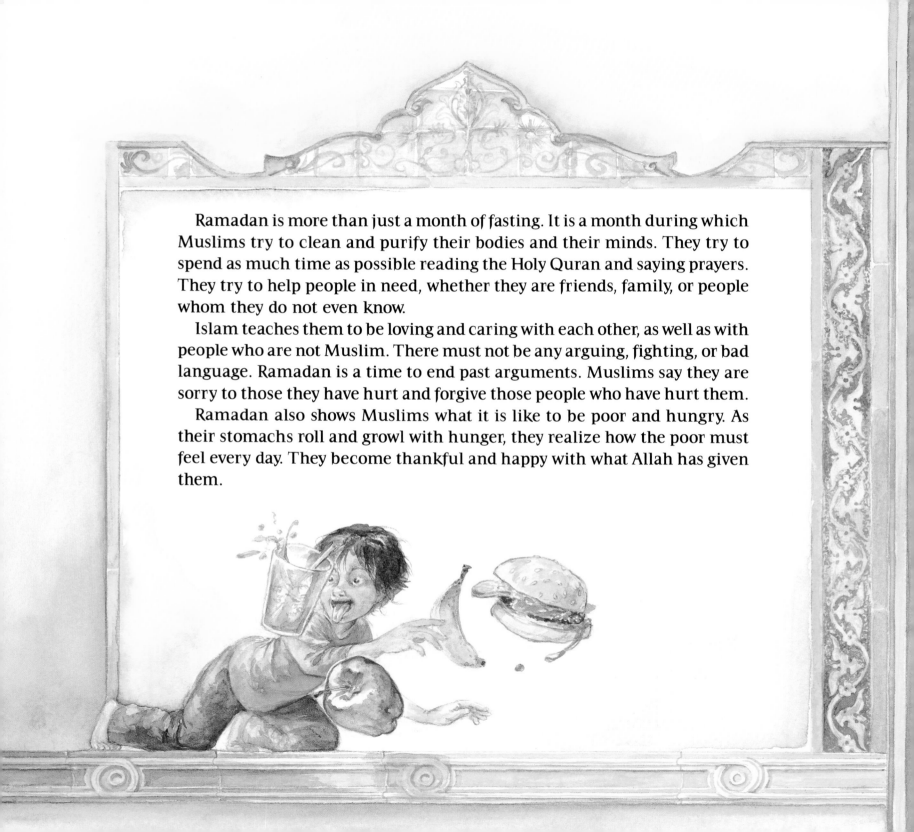

Because fasting requires a strong mind and body, not everyone is supposed to do it. Old people and young children are excused from fasting because their bodies are not strong enough to stay healthy without food. It is important for them to get proper nutrition. Sometimes, however, children will fast for half a day or fast a few days out of the month. This gives them a chance to learn the holy tradition of Ramadan and also makes them feel as grown up as everyone else.

People who are sick and people who are traveling are also not allowed to fast because they need a lot of energy and rest. Fasting could harm them instead of help them. Pregnant women are not allowed to fast either, because they need to eat throughout the day to keep themselves and their unborn babies in good health.

As the sun begins to slide down the sky and slip into the horizon, Hakeem and his brother and sister set the table. His mother is busy in the kitchen, preparing the dinner feast.

When the sun finally sets, the family breaks their fast with a meal that is called *Iftar*. Muslims start the Iftar by eating a date and thanking Allah for having given them the strength to fast. This is the same way Prophet Muhammad and his followers broke their fasts more than a thousand years ago in the open deserts of Arabia.

Once Muslims have broken their fasts and had a drink, they wash up so that they can perform the evening prayer called *Maghrib*. Once again, Hakeem's father leads the family as they pray to Allah in neat, little rows.

By the time they finish their prayers, the sun has disappeared. The pale, glowing moon is visible in the night sky, surrounded by hundreds of sparkling stars. Hakeem's family gathers around the dining table for a large dinner.

They eat juicy beef, tangy chicken, and fried fish on plates of steaming rice. Dad serves his special garden salad which is filled with plump tomatoes, sweet carrots, crispy lettuce, and Greek feta cheese. Sometimes they have tasty stews with oven-baked bread. The children wash away their thirst with gallons of chilled punch and lemonade, Hakeem's favorite.

As Hakeem's family sits and enjoys their feast, they laugh and talk about their day, telling each other funny or interesting stories.

When they have finished eating, they thank Allah for having blessed them with the good health to survive their fast and for the food that breaks their fast. Once Iftar has been finished, all the hunger pangs and the thirst are forgotten. The special dinner certainly makes waiting all day worthwhile.

After a few hours Hakeem's family goes to the mosque. A mosque is the place where Muslims pray and worship Allah, as the Christians do in a church and the Jews do in a synagogue. During Ramadan, there are special prayers at night in the mosque. These prayers are called the *Taraweeh* prayers.

Hundreds of people from all over the city come to pray and share in the Ramadan spirit. Everyone brings some food for the poor people who have not been able to break their fasts properly.

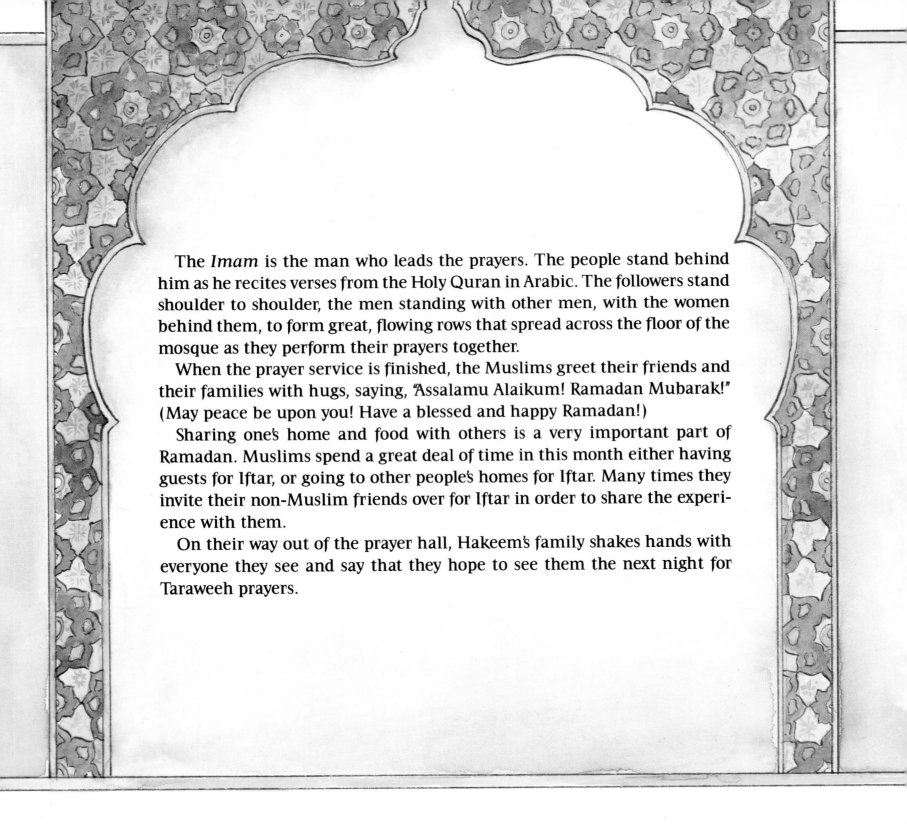

The *Imam* is the man who leads the prayers. The people stand behind him as he recites verses from the Holy Quran in Arabic. The followers stand shoulder to shoulder, the men standing with other men, with the women behind them, to form great, flowing rows that spread across the floor of the mosque as they perform their prayers together.

When the prayer service is finished, the Muslims greet their friends and their families with hugs, saying, "Assalamu Alaikum! Ramadan Mubarak!" (May peace be upon you! Have a blessed and happy Ramadan!)

Sharing one's home and food with others is a very important part of Ramadan. Muslims spend a great deal of time in this month either having guests for Iftar, or going to other people's homes for Iftar. Many times they invite their non-Muslim friends over for Iftar in order to share the experience with them.

On their way out of the prayer hall, Hakeem's family shakes hands with everyone they see and say that they hope to see them the next night for Taraweeh prayers.

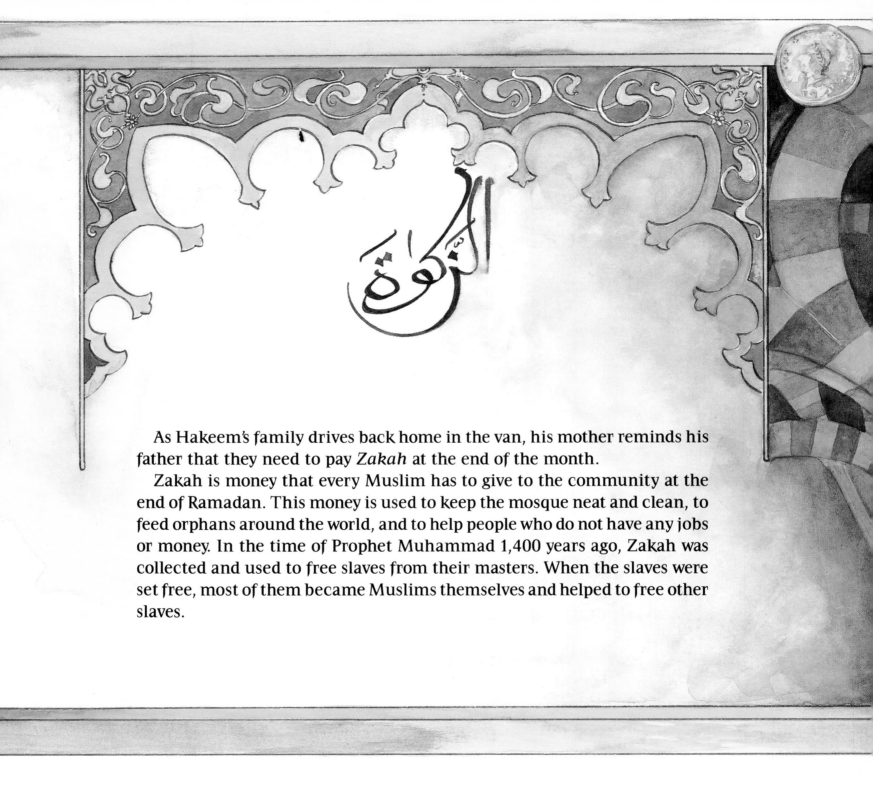

As Hakeem's family drives back home in the van, his mother reminds his father that they need to pay *Zakah* at the end of the month.

Zakah is money that every Muslim has to give to the community at the end of Ramadan. This money is used to keep the mosque neat and clean, to feed orphans around the world, and to help people who do not have any jobs or money. In the time of Prophet Muhammad 1,400 years ago, Zakah was collected and used to free slaves from their masters. When the slaves were set free, most of them became Muslims themselves and helped to free other slaves.

When the month of Ramadan draws nearer to its end, Hakeem and his family return to the hills and scan the skies every night, searching for the new moon. The sliver of the new moon will tell them that Ramadan has ended and that the next day is *Eid ul-Fitr*. Eid ul-Fitr is a holiday during which Muslims celebrate their success at fasting in Ramadan.

On this holiday, all the Muslims from far and near gather at a public place, such as a hall or a park. Everyone arrives with his or her family and wears their best clothes.

There are Muslims from all over the world in Hakeem's community. They come from Pakistan and Palestine, from Spain and Somalia, from Australia and Algeria, and from Norway and Nigeria. They all speak different languages and have their own style of dressing. They come in different shapes, different colors, and different sizes.

Even though they have different faces and come from separate places, they share the same religion and beliefs. When Hakeem sees all these Muslims from around the world, he feels a sense of family and brotherhood with them because he understands that Islam is a religion for anybody and everybody — it does not matter where you are from or what you look like.

Together, in one large group, the Muslims will perform a special Eid prayer and then listen to the Imam's sermon. When the sermon ends, they will all rise to their feet and embrace one another, saying, "Eid Mubarak!" This means "Have a happy and blessed Eid."

The Muslims look for their family and friends, but they are so happy that they also hug people who they may not even know. They thank Allah for making them healthy enough to fast, and they pray that He will keep them healthy enough to fast the next year.

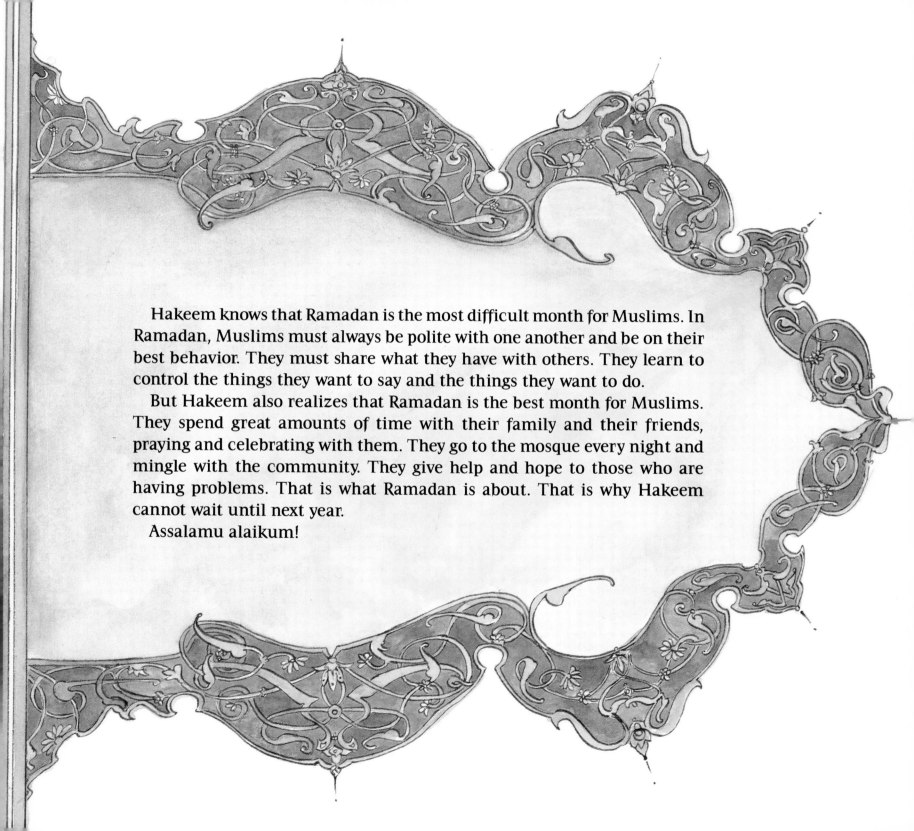

Hakeem knows that Ramadan is the most difficult month for Muslims. In Ramadan, Muslims must always be polite with one another and be on their best behavior. They must share what they have with others. They learn to control the things they want to say and the things they want to do.

But Hakeem also realizes that Ramadan is the best month for Muslims. They spend great amounts of time with their family and their friends, praying and celebrating with them. They go to the mosque every night and mingle with the community. They give help and hope to those who are having problems. That is what Ramadan is about. That is why Hakeem cannot wait until next year.

Assalamu alaikum!

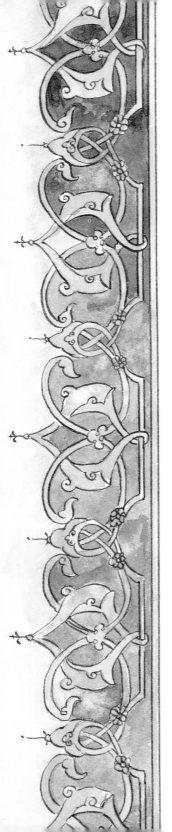

GLOSSARY

ALLAH   The Islamic name for God.

ASSALAMU ALAIKUM   The Islamic greeting, which means 'May peace be upon you.'

EID UL-FITR   The holiday following the end of Ramadan during which Muslims celebrate successful fasting.

EID MUBARAK   The Islamic greeting during Eid celebrations, which means "Have a happy and blessed Eid."

FAJR   The first of the five daily Islamic prayers, performed after Suhur.

FASTING   Refraining from eating or drinking for a certain period of time.

HIRA   The cave where Muhammad was first revealed the Quran.

IFTAR   The meal Muslims eat at sunset to break their fast during Ramadan. It usually begins with a date.

IMAM   The man who leads the prayers.

ISLAM   A religion of over one billion people who follow the teachings of Prophet Muhammad and worship Allah.

LUNAR CALENDAR   A calendar that calculates months by using the moon instead of the sun.

MAGHRIB   The fourth of five daily prayers, performed after Iftar.

MOSQUE   The place where Muslims go to worship.

MUHAMMAD   The last Prophet of Allah, who was sent the Quran 1,400 years ago.

MUSLIM   A person who follows the religion of Islam.

QURAN   The religious book of the Muslims that was revealed to Muhammad.

RAMADAN   The holy month of fasting for Muslims. The ninth month of the Muslim lunar calendar.

RAMADAN MUBARAK   The Islamic greeting during Ramadan, which means "Have a happy and blessed Ramadan."

SUHUR   The early meal that Muslims eat before sunrise to start their fasts during Ramadan.

SYNAGOGUE   The place where Jewish people go to worship.

TARAWEEH   Special night-time prayers performed only during Ramadan.

ZAKAH   Money that every earning Muslim must give to the community every year. It is generally given at the end of Ramadan.